CLEMENT C. MOORE

THE NIGHT BEFORE CHRISTMAS

ILLUSTRATED BY LEONARD WEISGARD

BARNES
&NOBLE
BOOKS
NEW YORK

'Twas
the night before
Christmas,
when all through
the house

Not
a creature
was stirring,
not even
a mouse;

The stockings
were hung by
the chimney
with care,
In hopes
that St.
Nicholas
soon would
be there;

The children

all snu

While vision

danced

were nestled

in their beds,

of sugar-plums

through their

heads;

And Mamma in
   her 'kerchief,
   and I in my cap,
Had just settled
   our brains
   for a long winter's nap,
When out on the lawn
   there arose such
   a clatter,
I sprang from my bed
   to see what was
   the matter.
Away to the window
   I flew like a flash,
Tore open the shutters
   and threw up
   the sash.

The moon on
the breast of
the new-fallen snow
Gave a lustre of
mid-day to
objects below,
When, what to my
wondering eyes
did appear,
But a miniature
sleigh, and
eight tiny rein-deer,

With a little old driver
        so lively and quick,
I knew in a moment
        he must be St. Nick.
More rapid than eagles
        his coursers they came,
And he whistled, and shouted,
        and called them by name:
"Now, Dasher! now, Dancer!
        now, Prancer and Vixen!
On, Comet! on, Cupid!
        on, Donder and Blixen!
To the top of the porch!
        to the top of the wall!
Now dash away! dash away!
        dash away, all!"

As leaves that before
the wild hurricane fly,
When they meet with an obstacle
mount to the sky,

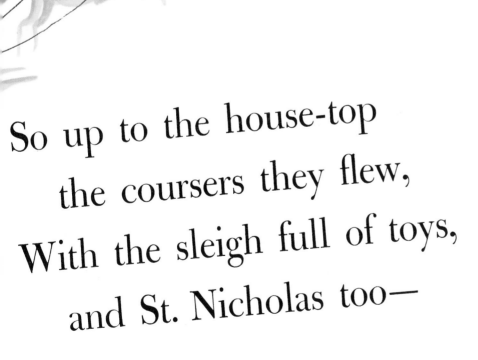

So up to the house-top
the coursers they flew,
With the sleigh full of toys,
and St. Nicholas too—

And then in a twinkling,

   I heard on the roof

The prancing and pawing

   of each little hoof.

As I drew in my head,

   and was turning around,

Down the chimney St. Nicholas

   came with a bound.

He was dressed all in fur,
from his head to his foot,
And his clothes were all tarnished
with ashes and soot;
A bundle of toys he had
flung on his back,
And he looked
like a peddler
just opening
his pack.

His eyes—how

his dimple

His cheek

his nos

ney twinkled!

ow merry!

vere like roses,

ke a cherry!

His droll little mouth

vas drawn up like a bow,

And the beard

on his chin

vas as white as

the snow;

The stump of a pipe
he held tight in his teeth,
And the smoke it encircled
his head like a wreath;
He had a broad face
and a round little belly
That shook when he laughed,
like a bowl full of jelly.

He was chubby and plump,
a right jolly old elf,
And I laughed when I saw him
in spite of myself;
A wink of his eye and
a twist of his head
Soon gave me to know
I had nothing to dread;

He spoke not a word, but went straight to his work, And filled all the stockings; then turned with a jerk, And laying his finger aside of his nose, And giving a nod, up the chimney he rose.

He sprang to his sleigh,
to his team gave a whistle,
And away they all flew
like the down of a thistle.

But I heard him exclaim
ere he drove out of sight—

"Happy Christmas to all

and to all a Good Night!"

ISBN 0-7607-0685-9
Printed and bound in China
M 9 8 7 6 5 4 3 2 1